Ellen
HOBO JUNGLE

DOROTHY JOAN HARRIS

PENGUIN
CANADA

PENGUIN CANADA
Published by the Penguin Group
Penguin Books, a division of Pearson Canada, 10 Alcorn Avenue, Toronto, Ontario, Canada
M4V 3B2
Penguin Books Ltd, 80 Strand, London WC2R 0RL, England
Penguin Putnam Inc., 375 Hudson Street, New York, New York 10014, U.S.A.
Penguin Books Australia Ltd, 250 Camberwell Road, Camberwell, Victoria 3124, Australia
Penguin Books India (P) Ltd, 11, Community Centre, Panchsheel Park,
New Delhi – 110 017, India
Penguin Books (NZ) Ltd, cnr Rosedale and Airborne Roads, Albany,
Auckland 1310, New Zealand
Penguin Books (South Africa) (Pty) Ltd, 24 Sturdee Avenue, Rosebank 2196, South Africa

Penguin Books Ltd, Registered Offices: 80 Strand, London WC2R 0RL, England

DESIGN: MATTHEWS COMMUNICATIONS DESIGN INC.
MAP ILLUSTRATION: SHARON MATTHEWS
INTERIOR ILLUSTRATIONS: RON LIGHTBURN

First published, 2002

3 5 7 9 10 8 6 4

Publisher's note: This book is a work of fiction. Names, characters, places, and incidents either are the product of the author's imagination or are used fictitiously, and any resemblance to actual persons living or dead, events, or locales is entirely coincidental.

Manufactured in Canada

NATIONAL LIBRARY OF CANADA CATALOGUING IN PUBLICATION DATA

Dorothy Joan Harris, 1931–
Hobo jungle: Ellen
(Our Canadian girl)
ISBN 0-14-100270-0

1. Depressions—1939—British Columbia—Vancouver—Juvenile fiction.

I. Title. II. Series.

PS8565.A6483H58 2002 jC813'.54 C2001-902666-8
PZ7.H24125Hob 2002

Visit Penguin Books' website at **www.penguin.ca**

For
Rachel Emily and Alan Douglas

Yukon
Northwest Territories
Nunavut
British Columbia
Alberta
Saskatchewan
Manitoba
Ontario

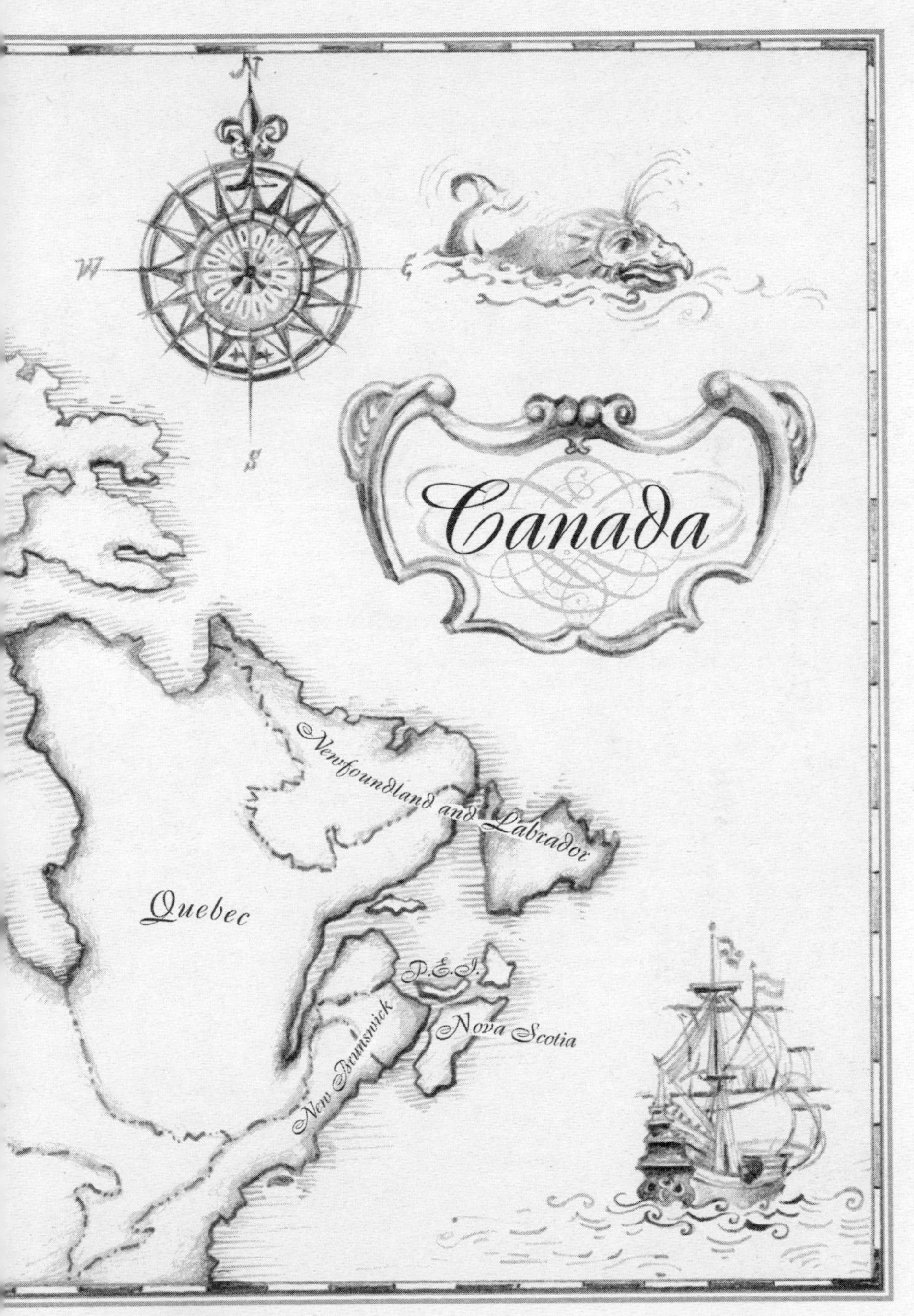

Marks the location of the story

Meet Ellen

You perhaps know some people who have lost their jobs. That's something that is very hard on them, and on their families. But nowadays there are usually other jobs available. And there is Employment Insurance and Welfare to help.

Now try to imagine a time when three out of four fathers had no jobs and no prospects of finding one. That is what it was like in the 1930s, during the Depression. Thousands of Canadian families did not have enough money for food or heat or clothes or anything else. Girls like Ellen, in this book, could never hope to go and buy a new dress to start school. So they let down hems on dresses that were too short, or reused material from other dresses to sew themselves something new. To entertain themselves they read books from public libraries, which were free, or listened to the radio, if they had one. There was no television then, no computer games. There were movies, but they cost money, and girls like Ellen couldn't afford to go.

Like Ellen, many people back then found it hard to understand just what had brought about the Depression. There were many causes—one was the fact that in the 1920s times had been very good, so people had spent money freely, buying whatever they wanted. Factories were going at full speed to provide the cars, clothes, toasters, and other things that people wanted. The stock market was booming, and many, many people hoped to get rich quickly on their stocks. Stock prices went up and up—until October 1929, when investors suddenly began to lose confidence. Then, investors wanted to sell their stocks—but since everyone wanted to sell at that point and nobody wanted to buy, the value of the stocks plummeted.

Those who had been rich were suddenly poor. But people who had never owned stocks were soon affected too. Since nobody was buying things, the factories that had been running at full speed began to shut down. This meant the factory workers no longer had jobs. And as more and more workers lost their jobs and had no money to spend, other places—like stores and banks—began to suffer too. Jobless men would sneak onto freight trains, hoping that they just might find some work somewhere along the line. But there was little work for them anywhere. No wonder the 1930s came to be called "**the Dirty Thirties**."

CHAPTER Nº 1

"I wish I still had a bedroom," said Ellen, using her teeth to snip the thread with which she was sewing. "Will I ever have my own room again?"

"Don't bite your thread," said her mother. "It's bad for your teeth. Here, use the scissors."

Ellen did as she was told. But her mother hadn't answered her question.

"I suppose . . . ," Ellen said slowly, "if Grandpa died, then I'd get his room."

"Hush, Ellen!" said her mother. "Don't even

say such a thing. It was very good of Grandpa Sanders to let us come and live with him when we just couldn't pay our rent any longer. There are lots of out-of-work families who would be happy to be living the way we are. We're very lucky."

But Ellen didn't feel lucky. She hadn't felt lucky for months, not since her father had lost his job at the bank. Now they were living in Grandpa Sanders's small house, which had only two bedrooms—so Ellen had to sleep on the couch at night.

And there were other things that Ellen would have liked to complain about. Like having to always be quiet so as not to disturb Grandpa. Like never having a nickel for an ice cream cone on a hot day. Like losing all her friends from her old neighbourhood. There wasn't anyone her age to play with on Grandpa's street. No one at all. And no way to go back to see her old friends, on the other side of Vancouver, since there wasn't any money for bus fare either.

Ellen picked out a thread from the used ones laid out on the dining-room table and started on another seam. She wouldn't have minded helping her mother to sew if they had been working on something pretty for her to wear. But this was material from one of her grandmother's dresses that her mother was using to make a dress for her. Her dead grandmother. That was sort of spooky, Ellen thought.

Ellen wriggled in her seat. When she finished this seam she'd say she had to go to the bathroom again. Ellen had one of her library books stashed in there. Or maybe her mother would even let her make some lemonade. If there was any sugar, that is . . .

Suddenly, outside, Ellen heard a rumbling.

"What's that?" she said. "It sounds like a truck. Are we getting something delivered?"

"Of course not," said her mother. "What would we be getting?"

But Ellen had already dropped her sewing and run to the window. "It is a truck," she told her mother. "An old pickup truck with some baskets in the back. Oh—and there's a girl getting out. And she's got a little suitcase with her. She's going up to the house next door! Look!"

By now Ellen's mother had come to stand by the window too. "Yes, I see," she said.

"She looks just about my age! Do you think she's coming to live there? Oh Mom, can I go out and ask her if she's going to be living there?"

"Oh, I don't think so, Ellen. Let's wait just a bit—we mustn't be nosy."

"I'm not being nosy. I'm just being friendly. Oh-h-h, it's too late." Ellen's face fell. "She's gone in now. And the man who was driving has gone in too."

"Never mind, dear," said her mother. "If she is living next door you'll have lots of chances to talk to her."

Her mother went back to her chair in front of the old treadle sewing machine. Ellen stayed at the window. She saw the man who had been driving return to the truck and take a basket from the back. It seemed to be full of potatoes, and she pressed her nose against the window to see better.

"Ellen, now you *are* being nosy," her mother cautioned her. "Come and finish that bit of basting, please. I'm ready to do it on the machine."

With one last glance out the window Ellen went back to her chair. She took a few more long stitches—too long, Ellen suspected, but she didn't stop to correct them. "There. It's done," she said.

She handed the slightly crumpled material to her mother and then picked up a dress that was lying on the table. The dress was one of hers, a flowered one that she liked and had worn a lot. But it was much too short for her now, so her mother had let down the hem. Only, because she'd worn it so much, the rest of the dress was faded. Only the fabric of the hem was still bright. Ellen held it up and frowned at it.

"This dress looks weird now, with a bright strip all around the bottom," she said.

She walked into the bedroom with it and held it up against her as she stared into the mirror. She was still frowning when she came back to the dining room.

"Isn't there some way that we can fade the bright part?" she asked her mother. "Maybe leave the dress out in the sun? If we covered the old part and just left the hem showing, then maybe it would get faded too."

Her mother smiled at the suggestion. "I don't think that would work, really."

"Well, we'll have to do *something*. I don't want to look weird and have kids laugh at me. Especially since I have to start a new school here."

"Oh Ellen, I'm sure you won't be laughed at," her mother said gently. "I'm sure there will be lots of other girls in dresses with let-down hems. And you'll have this new one we're making—you can wear that for your first day."

Ellen was still looking unhappily at her dress. "But Mom . . . ," she said, "Daddy's working again, now that he's found that cleaning job at the factory. So how come we still don't have any money for things?"

She held the dress up against her as she stared into the mirror.

"Well, he doesn't make very much at the factory, even though it's hard work," her mother explained. "And we have to buy food, and give Grandpa Sanders money for the electricity and taxes and all the other house expenses."

"I don't see why we have to do that," Ellen grumbled. She kept her voice low and glanced over at the door to the living room. Grandpa Sanders was in there, reading the newspaper. "After all, he'd still have to pay taxes and electricity, whether we were here or not."

"But we *want* to help with the expenses," said her mother. "Neither Daddy nor I want him to feel we're taking advantage of him."

"Is that what he thinks we're doing?" said Ellen. "Is that why he's often cross, especially with me? I don't think he likes me much," she added.

"Oh Ellen, of course he likes you," her mother assured her. "It's just that he's not used to having us all living with him. And besides, his arthritis is really painful some days—that's why he's cranky."

Her mother started the sewing machine going

again, and its noisy whirr drowned out any more talk. There was lots more Ellen would have liked to ask about. She still didn't understand what the Depression was all about. People talked about the Depression all the time (the word always had a big black capital D in Ellen's mind). But she still couldn't understand just *why* everyone was so poor now.

Her mother had told her that it had all started ten years ago, back in 1929, when the stock market had crashed in New York. But that didn't seem like much of an explanation to Ellen. Why should something that happened in New York make all of Canada so poor? Ellen's father had never owned any stocks. And the bank he'd worked for was still standing—there just wasn't a job for him any more.

"There, that's the top done." Her mother's voice interrupted her thoughts. "Come and let me try it on you."

Ellen went over and stood while her mother tried the top of her dress on her.

"That's fine," her mother said. "And the puffed sleeves will look really nice on you."

Her mother was trying to cheer her up, Ellen knew. Only Ellen wasn't in a mood to find anything nice.

"But it's such a dull colour," she said. "Just a dull old grey check—an old lady's colour."

Her mother made no reply to that, and Ellen went back to her chair.

Oh, if only some fairy godmother could change my life, she thought with a sigh.

CHAPTER No. 2

There was a knock at the back door.

Ellen jumped up, her sewing in her hand. *If this were a storybook, it would be my fairy godmother arriving*, she thought.

But when she opened the back door, it was just to a tall, thin man, in a plaid shirt and overalls. The shirt and overalls were frayed and grungy. This was no fairy godmother. This was just another out-of-work man. There were lots of them around.

Ellen's mother had come to the door too.

"Good morning, ma'am," the man said politely. "Is there some work I could do for you around here? I could sure do with something to eat."

"Oh . . . well, yes. I guess you could cut the grass," her mother answered. "Ellen will show you where the mower is."

Ellen looked at her mother in surprise. Cutting the grass was usually her job. But she didn't mind getting out of that, so she went outside, to the shed at the back of the yard, and showed the man where the old push-mower was. He thanked her and rolled it out of the shed.

Ellen went back inside.

"His clothes smell," she said to her mother.

"Well, of course they do," answered her mother. "If he's travelling about looking for jobs where could he wash? I'm sure he'd like to be clean. It's not his fault he's out of work."

"And I thought *I* was supposed to cut the grass today."

"I know you were. But he'll feel better if he does some work for us first. I'd feed him anyway, of course. I just keep thinking how lucky we are that Dad found a job at the factory."

"You mean . . . if he hadn't, *Dad* would be wandering around like that?" asked Ellen, horrified.

"Oh, I don't even want to think about that, honey," said her mother, picking up her sewing again. "I just know I can't say no to anyone who comes to the door hungry."

"You gave some food to a man a few days ago," Ellen said. "Maybe he told this man to come here."

Her mother sighed. "Perhaps he did. I've heard that men looking for a meal put a mark on a house where people are kind, to let others know."

"A mark? What kind of mark?"

"I've no idea."

"Can I go have a look? Or maybe ask this man?"

"No, of course not. Just let him cut the grass."

It didn't take the man long to finish the job. The yard wasn't very big. Ellen's mother had a sandwich ready for him, along with a glass of iced tea made from the tea left over from lunch.

The man thanked her politely and sat on the back steps to eat. It didn't take him long to eat, either. Ellen figured he must have been really hungry. He knocked at the door again to return the plate and glass, thanked her mother once more, and went off down the street.

"*Now* can I go outside and have a look?" Ellen asked. "A look for the mark?"

"Yes, if you want to," said her mother. "You *have* been sewing a long time—go get some fresh air."

Ellen put her needle back into her mother's sewing basket and hurried out into the yard. It was good to be outside, and the cut grass smelled sweet. She started to walk all around the house. Was it a painted mark? An X? She examined the front steps and then the back steps. But she couldn't see anything unusual.

And what would I do if I did find something? she asked herself. *Would I rub it out?*

There was something about living in a "marked" house that made her feel uncomfortable. But the picture in her mind of her own father going from house to house looking for a meal made her feel even worse. She knew she wouldn't rub it out.

Ellen was still searching for the mark, on her hands and knees now, when she heard the screen door slam on the house next door. The girl she'd seen getting out of the truck had come out.

She glanced over at Ellen's yard, saw Ellen on her knees, and came to the fence.

"Have you lost something?" she asked.

"Uh—no," said Ellen, scrambling to her feet. She came to the fence too. "Do you live in that house?"

"Yes," said the girl. She looked at Ellen for a moment. "Do you live *there?*"

"I do now," said Ellen. "We've moved in with my grandpa, my mom and dad and me. My name's Ellen Sanders."

"Oh," said the girl. "I'm Amy—Amy Takashima."

Ellen had been studying the girl, noting her shiny black hair and eyes. "Are you Japanese?"

"No. I'm Canadian," Amy said firmly. "I was born right in this house. I live here with my mom and dad."

"I haven't seen you before," said Ellen.

"No, I was at my uncle's place. He's a farmer, he grows vegetables and stuff. I was helping pick strawberries."

"That sounds like fun. Can you eat as many as you want?" Ellen asked.

"Well, yes. But it's not really fun. It's hard work."

They stared at each other for a moment. Then Ellen said, "I'm glad you're back now. I haven't seen any other kids on this street. Uh . . . would you like to come over? We could play ball or something."

Amy looked doubtful. "I don't think your grandfather likes children to play ball in his yard."

Ellen considered this. "Probably not," she said. "Mom says it's his arthritis that makes him cranky, but I don't think he likes children much." She sighed. "Everything was much nicer before, when we had a house of our own."

"Where was your house?" asked Amy.

"Over on the other side of Vancouver. That was before my father lost his job, before the Depression." Ellen gave another sigh. "I don't really understand what the Depression is, do you?"

"No, just that there are lots and lots of people without jobs. My dad says he's lucky he works with my uncle. My dad sells the vegetables from his truck, and people always need vegetables." She paused. "Would you like to come over to my yard? There's a swing in our tree."

"Oh, sure," said Ellen.

Ellen went carefully around the fence to reach Amy's yard. Amy let her have the first swing. After sitting so long it felt good to swing as high as she could. She could imagine herself swinging right up over the tree, flying away from Grandpa Sanders's street. Away . . . away . . .

Ellen and Amy took turns for quite a while. But then Amy said, "I'll have to go in now. I have to do my practising."

"Oh . . ." Ellen let her disappointment show. "Practising what?"

"The piano. I didn't do any at my uncle's."

"You have a *piano?*" said Ellen. "Lucky you! At my old school I was taking group piano lessons. There were six of us in the class, so we only got a little time each to play. And I've never had a piano to practise on."

"Oh . . ." Amy pulled a face. "I *have* to practise, every day."

"What does it look like, your piano?"

"Oh, just ordinary," said Amy. "Would you like to see it?"

"Yes, please."

Ellen followed Amy into her house. In the kitchen, a small woman, with black hair like Amy's, was stirring something on the stove.

"Mom, this is Ellen," said Amy. "She's living next door now."

"Ah . . . ," said Amy's mother, giving Ellen a big smile. "You are living with Mr. Sanders?"

"Yes, he's my grandfather," said Ellen.

"Ellen wants to see our piano," Amy went on.

"Ah . . . good," said her mother. "You play?"

"Um . . . not very well," Ellen admitted. "Just a couple of pieces."

"Never mind, you go play," said Amy's mother.

Amy took Ellen into the living room, where a big upright piano took up all of one wall. A music book lay open on the rack.

Ellen peered at the music book. "You're playing *that?*" she said. "It looks really hard."

"It is," said Amy. "What did you play at your lessons?"

"Only easy pieces."

Ellen sat down at the big piano and played the two pieces she'd learned. But playing them brought vivid memories of her old school, which made her rather sad. As soon as she'd finished the two pieces she stood up.

"I'd better go now," she said. "I didn't tell Mom where I was going."

When Ellen got home her mother was also standing by the stove.

"I met the girl who lives next door," Ellen told her. "Her name's Amy. And she has a piano! Could we have a piano some day?"

"Oh, Ellen, pianos cost a lot of money," her mother said.

"Well . . . maybe a guitar then? Something to sing with? You used to sing a lot," Ellen added.

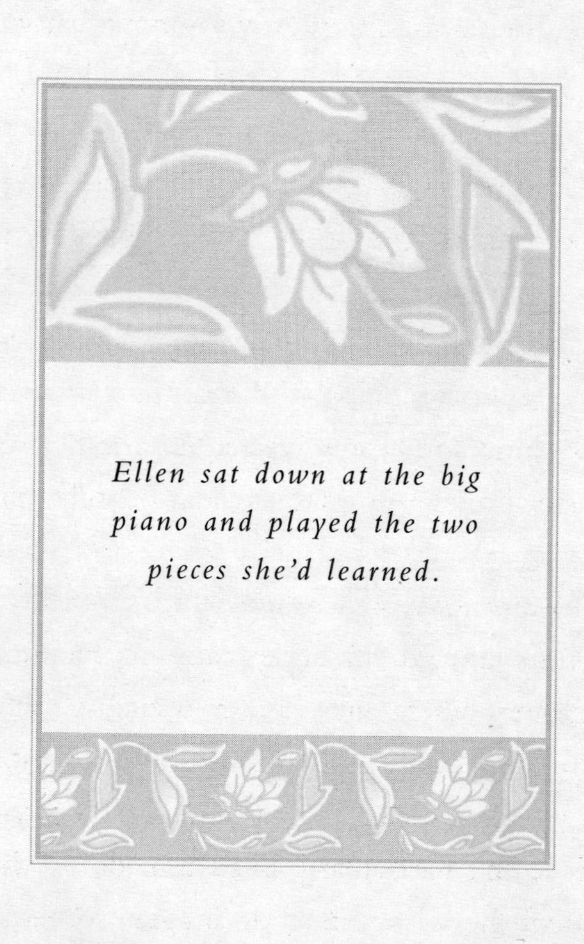

Ellen sat down at the big piano and played the two pieces she'd learned.

"Yes, well . . ." Her mother glanced quickly towards the living room. "Grandpa Sanders likes a quiet house, you know. Anyway, now that you're here you can start setting the table, please," she said. "I've cleared away the sewing."

Ellen spread a tablecloth over the table and then set out knives and forks and napkins in their napkin rings. Her mother insisted on clean tablecloths and proper napkins, just the way she had in their own house. Ellen, who had to help her scrub the washing, sometimes wished her mother wasn't so fussy about keeping up standards. Still, a nicely set table did make food taste better, Ellen had to admit—even when there wasn't much of it.

A little later Ellen's father came in. Ellen could remember when her father used to whistle around the house and make jokes. He used to pick up Ellen's long pigtails and say, "Giddy-up." Ellen hadn't particularly liked him doing that—but now she wished he'd do it again sometimes.

Tonight he came in quietly, said hello to Ellen, kissed Ellen's mother, and then sank tiredly into a chair in the living room. Grandpa Sanders handed him the newspaper, and he sat there reading it, without another word.

After supper they all sat in the living room. Grandpa Sanders turned on the radio for the news, which the grown-ups listened to with worried faces, especially if there was anything about Germany. Ellen couldn't understand why they should get so upset over things that were happening a world away. Then Grandpa Sanders listened to one of his favourite programs. But he turned the radio off as soon as the program was over. He was strict about how much electricity was used in the house.

Ellen spent every evening reading one of her many library books. She was glad that libraries, at least, were free. But by nine o'clock everyone was in bed, with Ellen on the couch, and all the lights were out.

That night Ellen lay wide awake in the dark for quite a while. From far off she could hear a train whistle. If only she could get on a train and go off to a different life somewhere. She didn't feel like going to sleep, and she longed to read a bit more of her book. *If I had a flashlight I could read in bed,* she thought.

But like everything else, flashlights cost money.

The next morning Ellen's father set off early, as usual. He no longer wore a suit, but he still insisted on wearing a tie with his shirt. And instead of carrying a lunchbox, he took his sandwiches in his old worn briefcase. Ellen went outside to wave goodbye to him, and she looked hopefully over at the house next door to see if Amy was about.

She'd been hoping to play with Amy again, but there was no chance for it that morning. Ellen's mother was doing the washing, and Ellen had to help. That meant spending the morning down in the dark basement, filling the washing machine, slivering the Sunlight soap into the water, and waiting while the clothes sloshed about in the tub. Then came the worst part: feeding the clothes through the wringer. Ellen was afraid of that wringer. After that, everything had to be rinsed and put through the wringer again. Ellen was always glad when it was time to carry the wet clothes up to the backyard.

She was helping her mother hang up the last sheet when she heard someone behind them.

"Good morning, ma'am."

It was the man who had cut the grass the day before.

"I noticed that your back steps need some fixing," he said. "I could do that for you if you've got some nails and a hammer."

"Why . . . yes, those steps do need fixing," said Ellen's mother. "And I'm sure we have a hammer. Ellen, go look in the shed."

Ellen came back with a hammer but no nails.

"Never mind," said the man. "I can make do with the nails that are here."

Ellen and her mother went back inside while the man began removing nails from the loose steps. Ellen watched him from behind the screen door. He had such a sad face, she thought.

"Where do you suppose he slept last night?" she whispered to her mother.

"Probably down by the railway yard," her mother answered. "That's where all the out-of-work men camp out. People call it the Hobo Jungle."

"Hobo Jungle?" said Ellen. "So is he a hobo?"

"I guess he is now."

"And is it really a jungle? Can I see it?"

"No, of course it's not a jungle—it's just an open patch of ground," said her mother. "And no, you can't see it. You mustn't ever go there."

"Why do they camp by the railway yard?"

"Because they all try to hitch rides on the trains, so they can look for work everywhere. Not that they're likely to find much," she added with a sigh.

"I wish I could go on a train somewhere," said Ellen.

Her mother didn't answer that. She picked up the empty laundry basket. "I'll go down and empty the washtubs," she said. "You could get on with that basting, Ellen. Then I could do the machine sewing before lunch."

Ellen went into the dining room to get her sewing. But she also picked up her library book and headed for the back porch. Out there she'd be able to sneak in a bit of reading, she thought.

She was singing a snatch of song under her breath as she sat down on the porch. The man working on the steps looked up and smiled.

"My daughter likes to sing that song," he told Ellen.

"You have a daughter?" said Ellen, surprised. "What's her name?"

"Willa. She was named after me—I'm Will."

"So . . . where is she?"

"Living with her grandparents."

"Oh. Like me," said Ellen. "We had to come

The man working on the steps
looked up and smiled.

and live with Grandpa Sanders when Dad lost his job at the bank. Did you lose your job?"

"You could say that. I was a farmer, on the prairies. But there's been a drought out there for years. Nothing grew, so we had nothing to sell, and we couldn't keep up the mortgage payments."

"Oh. Like us," Ellen said again. "We couldn't pay the rent on our house either. My dad has a job now, but it doesn't pay very much. So that's why I'm sewing this awful old material. It's the only way I'll get a new dress to wear to school." Ellen held her sewing up to show him. "See? It's such a dull old colour. It's from a dress that was my grandmother's, but she's dead now. So that makes it sort of spooky, too, don't you think? Dull and spooky."

The man—Will—couldn't answer right away because he had a couple of nails in his mouth. And as soon as he started hammering them in, Grandpa Sanders appeared at the door.

He peered out at Will without saying anything, then turned back to the kitchen. Ellen could hear him talking to her mother.

"I suppose you're going to feed that man," said her grandfather.

"Just a sandwich," her mother answered. "The bread is getting stale anyway."

"Humph!" said her grandfather. But he didn't try to stop her.

Ellen felt her own face growing red over Grandpa Sanders's rudeness. She was sure Will must have heard all that. So she jumped in with more questions.

"How old is your daughter, Mister Will?" she asked.

"She'll be ten now," he answered. "I haven't seen her for a year."

"Oh—I'm ten too," said Ellen. "So we're a lot alike. Does she like to sing? Does she have a piano?"

"No, no piano."

"The girl next door has a piano," said Ellen. "She let me try it. I wish we could have one. Or even a guitar. Anything that would make music."

"I used to play the banjo," Will told her.

"Did you? Have you still got it?"

"No. Everything got sold when they auctioned off the farm." Will's voice was quieter now, and sad.

"Oh. I'm sorry, Mister Will," said Ellen.

Will hammered in a few more nails, while Ellen sewed quietly for a minute. But only for a minute.

"Are you camping by the railway yard?" she asked.

Will nodded.

"And do you get rides on the train?"

"Well, we don't exactly 'get' rides on the train. We can't afford a ticket, so we have to try to jump into a boxcar when no one's looking."

"I've never been on a train," Ellen said longingly. "It must be wonderful to ride off to new places."

Will shook his head. "New places are sometimes no better than where you are," he said.

But Ellen was sure that somewhere new would

be better than where she was, sitting on her grouchy grandfather's porch, sewing a dress she didn't even like.

CHAPTER N° 5

Ellen was fully expecting to see Will turn up again the next day. But there was no sign of him that day, or the one after.

"I wonder where Mister Will is," she said to her mother.

"Mister Will?"

"Yes, the man who fixed our steps—his name is Will. I liked him."

"Did you?" said her mother. "I thought you said he was smelly."

"Well . . . he is. But he's nice to talk to. He

doesn't treat me like a kid. Do you think he's caught a train somewhere?"

"Quite likely," said her mother.

Amy, too, had gone off early that day, in the pickup truck. But towards supper the truck returned. And shortly afterwards Amy appeared at the door. She was carrying a basket of carrots and potatoes.

"My mother sent these over for you," she said to Ellen's mother. "We brought back too many from the farm."

"Oh my!" said Ellen's mother. "Are you sure you can't use them?"

"No, we have too many," said Amy.

"Well, thank you," said Ellen's mother. "And thank your mother for me, too."

"I will," said Amy.

"And . . . and can you maybe play outside after supper?" Ellen asked her.

"Sure," said Amy. "I'll be out in the backyard." And with that she slipped out the door again.

Ellen's mother put the basket on the counter.

"There's a lot here," she said sounding pleased. Then she turned to Ellen. "You didn't . . . you didn't drop any hints when you were next door, did you?"

"Hints about what?" said Ellen.

"Well . . . that we're having a hard time making ends meet."

"Oh Mom! Of course not!" said Ellen. "I just admired their piano, that's all."

"Good." Her mother started unpacking the basket. "There are a lot of carrots here. I wonder . . ." She turned to the cupboard and looked into the sugar canister. "Yes, we've got enough sugar. I think I'll use some of these to make a carrot cake."

"A cake!" said Ellen. It had been a long time since her mother had made a cake.

"Yes, we'll do it now, before supper. Start cleaning some of the carrots, Ellen, and I'll get out the grater."

The cake was soon made. It smelled so good when it came out of the oven, all puffed up and spicy. Ellen leaned over it and sniffed deeply.

"As soon as it's cooled I'll cut off some for you to take next door as a thank-you," said her mother.

Ellen's face fell. "Oh . . . do we have to? It's been so long since we've had a cake."

"I know. But we can't forget good manners, even if we are poor."

"Will you come with me then?" said Ellen. "You could meet Amy's mother—she's nice."

"Well . . . I don't know."

"Why not?" said Ellen. "You used to visit the neighbours all the time at our old house."

"Yes . . . I know." Her mother hesitated a moment. "Okay then. I will."

By the following day Ellen had decided they wouldn't be seeing Will again. But during the afternoon there was a knock at the door, and there he was.

"Hello, Mister Will!" said Ellen. "I thought maybe you'd decided to catch a train somewhere."

"No, I got a couple of days' work unloading trucks."

"Oh, that's good."

"Yes, it sure was. I made enough for a few square meals." He looked over Ellen's shoulder at her mother. "But I do appreciate the meals you gave me."

"I wish it could've been more," said her mother. "Would you like something now?"

"No, thank you. You save it for yourselves. I just came back to see if you'd like me to dig you a plot where you could plant some vegetables. Beans grow real fast. If you plant some now you'll have fresh beans in a few weeks."

"Oh . . . that sounds like a good idea," said her mother.

"Over there by the shed would be best," he

said. "The beans will get lots of sun there."

Will found a shovel in the shed and began to dig. Ellen went to her chair on the porch again. This time she was helping to take apart one of her mother's faded dresses. When it was all taken apart, her mother would sew it back together, with the un-faded side out.

It was a hot day, and she could see Will was soon mopping his forehead. She went inside, got a big glass of water, and took it over to him.

"Would you like a drink, Mister Will?" she asked. "You look hot."

"Yes, I am," he said. "Thanks."

He put down the shovel and sat on the grass. Ellen sat down beside him.

"I brought something to show you," he said, reaching into his shirt pocket. "It's a picture of my daughter."

"Oh, let's see," said Ellen.

The photo, rather dog-eared, showed a girl with light-coloured hair standing beside a farm-house. She was squinting into the sun, so it was hard to tell just what she looked like.

"That was taken a couple of years ago," said Will. "But it's all I have to remind me of home. You can't carry luggage with you when you're riding the rails."

"She looks pretty," said Ellen. "Her hair is curly, isn't it? I wish mine were curly. And blond like hers. Mine's so dull, just plain brown and straight." She studied the photo again. "I think she looks sort of like you."

"No, she looks like her mother, really," said Will. But he seemed pleased anyway. His face wasn't quite so sad when he was looking at the photo.

Ellen took the empty glass back to the porch and went on with her work, while Will went on with his digging. When he'd finished digging a good-sized plot he came to the porch and knocked on the back door.

"I've finished now, ma'am," he told Ellen's mother. "It's ready to plant any time."

"Yes . . . well, thanks," said her mother. "I have

to take Ellen's grandfather to the doctor downtown today, so I'll buy some seeds."

"And I'll say goodbye to you," Will went on. "I'm going to head back east a ways, see if there's maybe some work in the Okanagan."

"What sort of work?"

"Picking fruit. Not much pay but you do get to eat the fruit that's fallen on the ground."

"Well . . . goodbye then," said Ellen's mother.

"Good luck," added Ellen.

Ellen watched for a moment as Will trudged away. Her mother was bustling about getting ready, since Grandpa Sanders was already sitting impatiently in the hall.

"You'll be all right here alone, Ellen?" her mother asked as they left. "I'd take you with us but that's two more bus fares . . ."

"I'll be fine," said Ellen.

Ellen was actually looking forward to being on her own in the house. She'd be able to read as much as she wanted. She made herself a big jam sandwich and stood at the back door to eat it.

But while she was licking her fingers clean she spotted something out in the grass.

She went out to look. It was Will's photo of his daughter.

Ellen snatched it up. It must have fallen out of his pocket. This was terrible. The picture was all he had to remind him of his daughter and his home—he'd told her so. What on earth should she do?

She'd have to try and find him and give it back—before he got on a train for the Okanagan.

I know Mom said I was never to go near the Hobo Jungle, she thought. *But I have to. I just have to.*

CHAPTER No. 6

Ellen, still clutching the picture, hurried back into the house.

If I run really fast, she thought, *I can be back before Mom gets home. She'll never even have to know. It can't be far to the railway yard—the train whistle always sounds so close.*

She shut the door carefully behind her and set off, walking as fast as she could. She had never explored these streets before. The houses were all small, like Grandpa Sanders's. Once, she stopped to talk to a woman who was watering her grass, to ask if she was going in the right direction. It was turning out to be a lot farther than she had expected. She walked on and on. The houses started to look more rundown.

Then she heard a train whistle. Oh—could that be the train Will was planning to take? Was she going to miss him after all? She walked even faster, then broke into a run.

She rounded another corner, and then she could see the railway yard, and a long freight train standing in it. As she came closer she could see several small campfires there, with men sitting on the ground near them.

Ellen stood where she was for a moment, just looking. She was a little nervous at the thought of walking in among all those strange men. But still, the idea of a life riding the rails, eating around a campfire, moving on to somewhere new when you felt like it—it all sounded very exciting. Better than being stuck in one place, especially a place where you weren't really wanted . . .

"What are *you* doing here?" said a voice beside her.

Ellen gave a startled jump. She hadn't noticed the man who had come up behind her. He wore a torn shirt and filthy pants with a rope for a belt, and his hair was dirty and matted.

"Have you just come here to gawp at us? We're not animals in a zoo, you know!"

"No . . . I know that," Ellen stammered. "I . . . I wasn't gawping."

"Then what are you doing here?"

"I've come to look for someone. He . . . he dropped something at our house. I wanted to—"

Ellen broke off there, as she saw the great freight train start to move.

"Oh! Oh gosh!" she cried. Was that the train that Will was planning to jump on? Was she too late to find him?

But before the train had gone very far there was a dreadful shriek. It came from over by the moving train. There were shouts, and the train ground to a stop.

Immediately, the men sitting by the fires jumped up. They began to run towards the train. There was a lot of shouting as they crowded towards one spot.

"What's happened?" Ellen asked.

But the man who'd been questioning her was running too. She followed him, towards the crowd of men. There she heard someone say, "Another accident. Another guy falling off the train."

"Oh!" said Ellen. "Oh—who is it? Is it a tall, thin man?"

The man she'd been following turned to face her then.

"Get out of here!" he told her. "Go home. You don't belong here."

By now that was just what Ellen longed to do. She'd gotten close enough to catch sight of someone lying on the ground. Was it Will? She didn't think so; the hurt man wasn't wearing overalls. But she could see blood. Any illusions she'd had about the hoboes' carefree life had disappeared.

But she still had Will's photograph clutched in her hand.

"No!" she said loudly. "No, I have to find Mister Will first."

In spite of her brave words, Ellen was truly scared now. All around her was a crowd of rough men, pushing forward and paying no attention to the small girl in their midst.

She tried calling out, "Mister Will! Mister Will! Does anybody know Will?"

Nobody so much as looked at her.

"Mister Will!" she called again.

Her voice was lost in the shouting and talking. But then, suddenly, she felt her arm being grasped. There was Will, beside her.

"Ellen! What are *you* doing here?" he asked.

"Oh, Mister Will . . ." Ellen was so relieved she could hardly speak for a minute.

She held out the photograph. "It's this," she said at last. "The picture of your daughter. You must have dropped it. It was in the grass where you were digging."

Will didn't take it right away. He seemed too stunned.

"You came here, all by yourself?" he asked.

"I . . . I had to. I had to get it back to you. Mom and Grandpa Sanders went downtown to the doctor, and you said you were leaving today. I was afraid you were on that train. Here—here's your picture."

He took it from her then, and he looked at it for a long minute. "Come on," he said at last. "We have to get you home."

"But what about the train you were leaving on?"

"Never mind that," he said. "Come on."

Ellen, with Will beside her now, retraced her

steps back to her own street. Will walked so quickly that she had to half run to keep up. Ellen was too out of breath to talk, and Will didn't say much, just, "You shouldn't have come. You shouldn't have done that."

When they reached her street, he stopped.

"You're home now," he told her. "You'll be all right now. And . . . thank you for my picture."

He turned and strode off, back towards the railway yard. Ellen watched him for a few seconds, then ran for home.

Her mother was sure to be home by now, she figured, so she was in for a scolding. But that was okay. After all the noise and fear at the Hobo Jungle, the small stucco bungalow seemed a wonderful, safe place.

As she neared the house she could see her mother standing at the front door, peering out. Even at a distance Ellen could see the worry on her face. She ran harder, up the steps, and into her mother's arms.

"Ellen! Where have you been?" her mother

exclaimed, hugging her tightly.

"Oh Mom, I'm sorry!" Ellen sobbed. "But you see, Will dropped the photo of his daughter—the only one he had. So I just had to get it back to him."

"You mean—you went to the *railway yard?* To the Hobo Jungle?"

"Yes. I know you told me never to go there . . . only I had to go. But oh, Mom, I'm so glad to be home. I'm so glad to *have* a home."

They had moved inside as they talked. And there was Grandpa Sanders in the hallway. He looked worried too.

"You're back then? Safe and sound?" he said.

"Oh, Grandpa . . ." Impulsively, Ellen detached herself from her mother and went over to give him a hug too. "I'm sorry I upset you."

"Humph!" said her grandfather, trying to look cross. "Well—don't do it again."

"You'll have to be punished, you know," her mother told her. "You disobeyed me."

Ellen nodded. "I know. Will I get a spanking?"

"Much worse than that," said her mother.

Ellen looked up, startled. What did she mean?

"No library books, not for a whole week," her mother said. "I'm going to put them all in my closet."

Ellen gave a quick glance at the book sitting on the chesterfield. And she was just getting to a good part, too.

"We were really upset, both of us," her mother said again.

Ellen didn't argue. "Okay," she said meekly.

CHAPTER No 8

Ellen wondered whether she'd get another scolding from her father when he got home. Maybe another punishment, too.

But her mother didn't even mention what Ellen had done. Her mother hardly ever talked about anything upsetting with her father, Ellen realized. Her father came in quietly, as usual, and took his place in his big chair. If he noticed that Ellen was not reading a book that evening, he didn't say anything.

What was unusual was that Grandpa Sanders

left the radio on for several programs. They listened to "The Jack Benny Program" and "Amos 'n' Andy," which were his favourites. But then they listened to "Baby Snooks" as well, which was Ellen's favourite. It was only after that one that he said, "Well, that's enough radio for one night." Ellen wondered whether maybe Grandpa Sanders did like her, after all.

As she lay on the chesterfield that night Ellen heard the train whistle again. But this time it didn't make her long to be somewhere else. Instead, she snuggled a little deeper into her pillow. It wasn't so bad being Ellen Sanders. She certainly didn't want to be one of the men camping at the railway yard, or trying to get on a train. And she was glad that *her* father wasn't tramping about looking for work with her picture in his pocket.

Even the next day she still felt glad to be Ellen. She helped her mother with the ironing (she just did the flat things, like napkins and handkerchiefs). She offered, all on her own, to cut the grass again. And she helped her mother plant the new garden with the beans she'd bought.

Amy came out of the house while they were doing the planting.

"Hi!" Ellen called to her. "Look! We're going to be farmers too."

Amy came over to the fence. "What are you planting?"

"Beans," said Ellen. "They're supposed to grow fast—do they?"

"Oh, sure," said Amy. "Just keep them watered." She watched them for a moment. "Um . . . don't plant them too deep," she said.

"Oh. Are these in too deep?" asked Ellen's mother.

"No, they'll be okay," said Amy.

"How fast will they grow?" asked Ellen. "Will we have some to pick next week?"

Amy laughed. "No, they don't grow that fast."

"Do you grow beans at your uncle's farm?" asked Ellen.

"Yes, lots. I'll bring you some next time I go."

"Oh, no," Ellen's mother said quickly. "You've brought us a lot already. But thank you anyway."

As they went back to their planting, Ellen's mother gave her a sharp look.

"You mustn't hint like that," she said in a low voice. "We don't need charity."

"But I wasn't hinting for anything," Ellen protested. "I was just talking. And—and anyway, *you* give food away. To Mister Will and anybody else who comes to the door."

"Yes . . . I know."

"So why isn't it okay if Amy's family gives us some beans?"

"Well, we've never had to take help before, you see. Ever since we were married, we've always prided ourselves on standing on our own two feet." Ellen's mother gave her a rueful smile. "I guess it's easier to be the giver."

"But somebody has to be the taker," Ellen pointed out.

"Yes, you're right," said her mother, ruffling

Ellen's hair for a moment before bending over to plant another seed. "I'll try to remember that."

Ellen spent most of the afternoon on the back porch, still carefully unpicking the seams on her mother's dress. But there was no book hidden under her sewing today. Her mother had hidden away all four of her library books. There was nothing to do but get on with the unpicking.

With her head bent over her work, she hadn't noticed anyone coming. So she gave a little start when she heard someone say, "Hello, Ellen."

"Oh!" Ellen jumped to her feet. "Mister Will! I thought . . . I thought you'd be gone by now."

"No," Will said. "I had to come and talk to your mother."

"Mom!" Ellen called from the kitchen door.

"Mister Will is here."

As soon as her mother appeared in the doorway Will began to apologize.

"I'm mighty sorry, ma'am, to have caused you any worry about Ellen yesterday," he said.

"Well . . . we *were* worried," said her mother. "But it wasn't exactly your fault."

"In a way it was. I dropped my photo."

"Not on purpose."

"No, that's true. Anyway, I wanted you to know I was sorry. And I wanted to bring something for Ellen." He held out a paper bag. "Here's a whole pile of onion skins. We eat a lot of onions at the camp—they're cheap."

"*Onion* skins?" said Ellen, staring at the bag but not taking it.

"Yes. They make a good yellow dye, you see," Will explained. "If you boil them up you can dye that dress of yours a prettier colour. And I made this for you, too." He took something from the bag and held it out. "It's a sort of pan pipe. I made it from the reeds that grow along by the tracks.

Will raised his hand in a salute. "I'll be going now. I have to see about getting to the Okanagan."

It's not the piano you wanted," he went on, "but you can play notes on it."

"Oh . . ." said Ellen. This time she took what he held out. "You made that for me?"

Will was smiling now. Ellen hadn't seen him smile before. She blew into one of the reeds and a thin note came out.

"I . . . I don't have anything for you," she said.

"You already gave me something," said Will.

"I did? You mean your photo?"

"No. You called me 'Mister Will.' It's been a long time since anyone called me 'Mister,'" he said sadly.

Ellen's mother put her hand on Will's arm. "Things will get better," she told him. "They have to get better soon. You'll see."

"Yes, ma'am," he said. "I sure hope so." He raised his hand in a sort of salute. "I'll be going now. I have to see about getting to the Okanagan."

Ellen and her mother watched him go. Ellen tried another note on her pipes.

"Things *will* get better," her mother repeated softly, and Ellen wasn't quite sure whether she'd said it to her daughter or to herself.

"Everything feels better already," said Ellen. "*I* feel better." *And even without a fairy godmother,* she thought.

Dear Reader,

Did you enjoy reading this Our Canadian Girl adventure? Write us and tell us what you think! We'd love to hear about your favourite parts, which characters you like best, and even whom else you'd like to see stories about. Maybe you'd like to read an adventure with one of Our Canadian Girls that happened in your hometown—fifty, a hundred years ago or more!

Send your letters to:

Our Canadian Girl
c/o Penguin Canada
10 Alcorn Avenue, Suite 300
Toronto, ON M4V 3B2

Be sure to check your bookstore for more books in the Our Canadian Girl series. There are some ready for you right now, and more are on their way.

We look forward to hearing from you!

Sincerely,

Barbara Berson
PENGUIN BOOKS CANADA

P.S. *Don't forget to visit us online at www.ourcanadiangirl.ca—there are some other girls you should meet!*

Canada's

1608
Samuel de Champlain establishes the first fortified trading post at Quebec.

1755
The British expel the entire French population of Acadia (today's Maritime provinces), sending them into exile.

1759
The British defeat the French in the Battle of the Plains of Abraham.

1776
The 13 Colonies revolt against Britain, and the Loyalists flee to Canada.

1783
Rachel

1812
The United States declares war against Canada.

1837
Calling for responsible government, the Patriotes, following Louis-Joseph Papineau, rebel in Lower Canada; William Lyon Mackenzie leads the uprising in Upper Canada.

1845
The expedition of Sir John Franklin to the Arctic ends when the ship is frozen in the pack ice; the fate of its crew remains a mystery.

1867
New Brunswick, Nova Scotia and the United Province of Canada come together in Confederation to form the Dominion of Canada.

1869
Louis Riel leads his Métis followers in the Red River Rebellion.

1870
Manitoba joins Canada. The Northwest Territories become an official territory of Canada.

1871
British Columbia joins Canada.

Timeline

1873 Prince Edward Island joins Canada.

1885 At Craigellachie, British Columbia, the last spike is driven to complete the building of the Canadian Pacific Railway.

1896 Gold is discovered on Bonanza Creek, a tributary of the Klondike River.

1898 The Yukon Territory becomes an official territory of Canada.

1905 Alberta and Saskatchewan join Canada.

1914 Britain declares war on Germany, and Canada, because of its ties to Britain, is at war too.

1917 In the Halifax harbour, two ships collide, causing an explosion that leaves more than 1,600 dead and 9,000 injured.

1918 As a result of the Wartime Elections Act, the women of Canada are given the right to vote in federal elections.

1939 Canada declares war on Germany seven days after war is declared by Britain and France.

1945 World War II ends conclusively with the dropping of atomic bombs on Hiroshima and Nagasaki.

1949 Newfoundland, under the leadership of Joey Smallwood, joins Canada.

1885
Marie-Claire

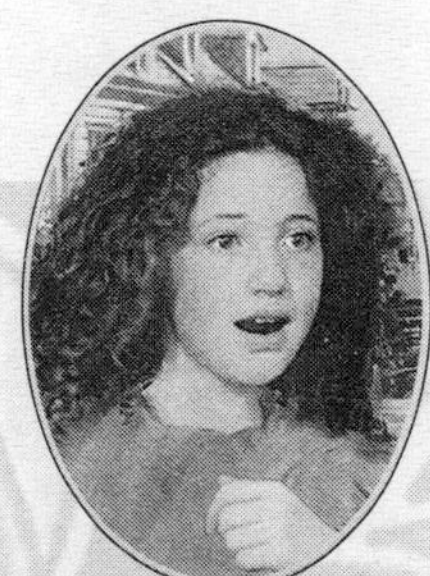

1896
Emily

1939
Ellen

Don't miss your chance to meet all the girls in the Our Canadian Girl series...

The story takes place in Montreal, during the smallpox epidemic of 1885. Marie-Claire, who lives in a humble home with her working-class family, must struggle to persevere through the illness of her cousin Lucille and the work-related injury of her father – even to endure the death of a loved one. All the while, Marie-Claire holds out hope for the future.

The year is 1917. Penny and her little sisters, Emily and Maggie, live with their father in a small house in Halifax. On the morning of December 6, Penny's father is at work, leaving Penny to get her sisters ready for the day. It is then that a catastrophic explosion rocks Halifax.

Ten-year-old Rachel arrives in northern Nova Scotia in 1783 with her mother, where they reunite with Rachel's stepfather after escaping slavery in South Carolina. Their joy at gaining freedom in a safe new home is dashed when they arrive, for the land they are given is barren and they don't have enough to eat. How will they survive?

Visit www.ourcanadiangirl.ca for free e-cards, sample chapters, activities, contests, and more!

Don't miss your chance to meet all the girls in the Our Canadian Girl series...

It's 1896 and Emily lives a middle-class life in Victoria, B.C., with her parents and two little sisters. She becomes friends with Hing, the family's Chinese servant and, through that relationship, discovers the secret world of Victoria's Chinatown.

When Elizabeth moves with her Planter family from New England to Nova Scotia's Annapolis Valley in 1762, she has a bad feeling about her new home. Elizabeth's family is given a farm that belonged to the Acadians, who have been deported by the English. Elizabeth soon discovers that someone is stealing their eggs and milk. And much worse, the Acadians – who must surely despise all Planters – are imprisoned in the barracks nearby.

Watch for more Canadian girls coming soon...

Visit www.ourcanadiangirl.ca for free e-cards, sample chapters, activities, contests, and more!